Dear Parent:
Your child's love of reading starts here!

Every child learns to read in a different way and at his or her own speed. Some go back and forth between reading levels and read favorite books again and again. Others read through each level in order. You can help your young reader improve and become more confident by encouraging his or her own interests and abilities. From books your child reads with you to the first books he or she reads alone, there are I Can Read Books for every stage of reading:

SHARED READING
Basic language, word repetition, and whimsical illustrations, ideal for sharing with your emergent reader

BEGINNING READING
Short sentences, familiar words, and simple concepts for children eager to read on their own

READING WITH HELP
Engaging stories, longer sentences, and language play for developing readers

READING ALONE
Complex plots, challenging vocabulary, and high-interest topics for the independent reader

ADVANCED READING
Short paragraphs, chapters, and exciting themes for the perfect bridge to chapter books

I Can Read Books have introduced children to the joy of reading since 1957. Featuring award-winning authors and illustrators and a fabulous cast of beloved characters, I Can Read Books set the standard for beginning readers.

A lifetime of discovery begins with the magical words **"I Can Read!"**

Visit www.icanread.com for information
on enriching your child's reading experience.

Night at the Museum: Battle of the Smithsonian: Larry's Friends and Foes
Night at the Museum: Battle of the Smithsonian ™ and © 2009 Twentieth Century Fox Film Corporation. All Rights Reserved.

Library of Congress Catalog card number: 2008942543
ISBN 978-0-06-171557-0

Typography by Rick Farley

❖

First Edition

I Can Read!

NIGHT AT THE MUSEUM™
BATTLE OF THE SMITHSONIAN

LARRY'S FRIENDS AND FOES

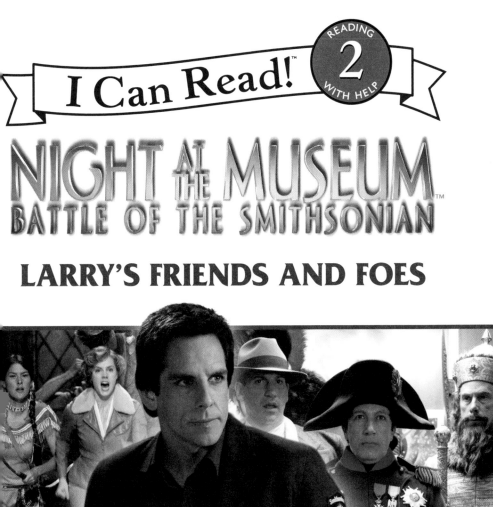

Adapted by Catherine Hapka
Based on the screenplay by
Robert Ben Garant & Thomas Lennon

HarperCollins*Publishers*

Larry Daley ran his own company.

But he missed his old job

at the Museum of Natural History

in New York City.

Larry was once the night guard there.

Larry also missed the statues
in the exhibits.

He knew their secret:

A magic Egyptian tablet
brought them to life each night!

One day Larry got some bad news.

The museum was going modern!

Most of the old statues were going

into storage at the Smithsonian Museum

in Washington, D.C.

"It's progress!" Dr. McPhee said.

Only some exhibits,
like Teddy Roosevelt
and Rexy the dinosaur,
were staying in New York.
The magic tablet would stay, too.

Larry knew what that meant.

Now the others wouldn't come alive!

They'd just be wax figures

and shabby stuffed animals.

Larry couldn't let that happen!

Larry sneaked into the Smithsonian.

He searched for his old friends.

But when he found them,

he got a big surprise.

The magic tablet was in one

of the boxes.

It made some Egyptian warriors

come to life.

They surrounded Larry.

The ruler of the warriors

was named Kahmunrah.

He knew all about the tablet.

Kahmunrah wanted to use its powers

to open the gate to the Underworld.

And he would stop at nothing

to get it away from Larry's friends!

Kahmunrah couldn't do it alone.

He needed some fighters to help him.

One of them was Napoleon.

He was a famous French general.

Napoleon was tough and smart,

but he wasn't very tall.

"You will now come with me,

little man!" he yelled at Larry.

"Little man?" Larry said, laughing.

Then there was Ivan the Terrible.

He was once the leader of Russia.

But Ivan explained that he wasn't

as terrible as everyone thought.

"It's not fair!" he said.

"My name really means

Ivan the Awesome!"

Al Capone helped Kahmunrah, too.
He was a famous American gangster.
"I'm mean, I'm lean,
and I'm going to rule the streets
forever!" Al bragged.

But Ivan knew the truth.

"You're going to end up bald, fat, and in jail," he told Al.

"What? No way!" Al said.

Luckily, Larry had plenty of help

in the fight against Kahmunrah

and his gang.

Larry had his old pals by his side.

Clever Sacajawea and Attila the Hun

were ready to help.

Larry made some new friends, too.

One of them was General Custer.

He was a famous army leader

during the Civil War.

But Custer wasn't very good

at planning ahead.

"Who needs a plan?" he said.

"Details are for the weak!"

Another new friend was named
Amelia Earhart.
She wasn't afraid of danger.
In fact, she loved it!

Larry had heard of Amelia.

"You were a pilot," he said.

"Not just any pilot," she said.

"I was the first woman

to fly across the Atlantic!"

Then there was Able the monkey.

He had been to space and back.

Able knew the museum

better than anybody!

Larry even met Abraham Lincoln.

Lincoln was a great president.

Now he was a great big statue.

Larry fought off Kahmunrah
with his flashlight.

All of Larry's old and new friends
helped Larry fight.

Soon, Kahmunrah's army was defeated!

Amelia gave Larry

and the New York exhibits

a ride home in her plane.

Then Larry put on his old uniform.

He was going to be a guard again.

Larry couldn't wait

to have his old job back!

GET REAL!

Teddy Roosevelt was a real person.

Did you know ... ?

FACT
When Teddy Roosevelt took office in 1901, he was 42 years old. He is still the youngest president in history.

FACT
Teddy was the first American to win the Nobel Peace Prize. He was also the first president to go underwater in a submarine, have a telephone in his home, and own a car!

FACT
Teddy loved wildlife. He famously refused to shoot a bear once on a hunt. That's why the teddy bear is named after him!

FACT
Some of Teddy's greatest accomplishments include building the Panama Canal and creating many national parks throughout the United States.